This Little Tiger book
belongs to:

_____

_____

_____

For my unicorn-fan friends, with thanks
— S S

For my mom, for always believing in me
— L M

LITTLE TIGER PRESS LTD,
an imprint of the Little Tiger Group
1 Coda Studios, 189 Munster Road, London SW6 6AW
www.littletiger.co.uk

First published in Great Britain 2019
This edition published 2020

Text copyright © Suzy Senior 2019
Illustrations copyright © Leire Martín 2019
Suzy Senior and Leire Martín have asserted their rights
to be identified as the author and illustrator of this work
under the Copyright, Designs and Patents Act, 1988

A CIP catalogue record for this book is available from the British Library

Printed in China • LTP/1800/3023/1019

2 4 6 8 10 9 7 5 3 1

UNICORN CLUB

SUZY SENIOR
LEIRE MARTÍN

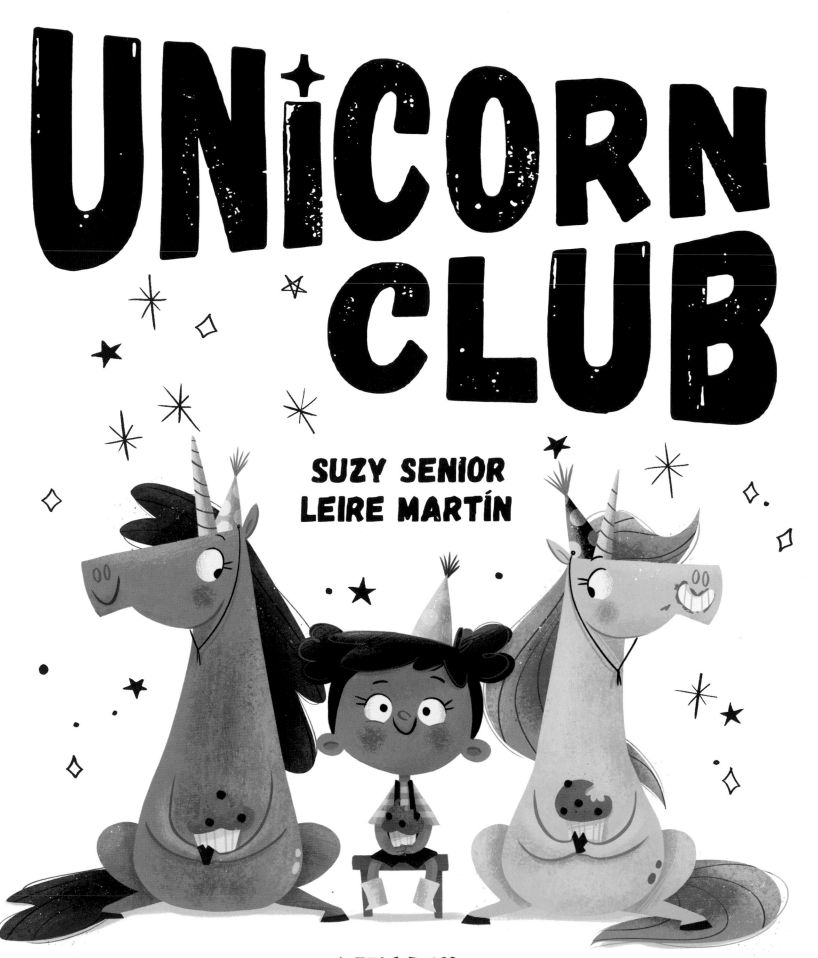

LITTLE TIGER

LONDON

Saturday morning felt full of excitement.
Saturday morning was sure to be great.
Amy was starting a unicorn fan club –
The poster was ready and stuck to the gate.

UNICORN CLUB is today in the tree house. Everyone welcome! At 20 past 10. Crafts and a snack and just 10p admission.

It said, in big letters, in shiny pink pen.

Amy was waiting, she hopped round the garden.
She nibbled a cookie and leaned on the gate.
No one was coming! The whole street was empty.
Her friends had forgotten – or else they were late.

Her Unicorn Club was a total disaster!
She finished her cookie and tried not to cry.
She pulled down the sign and went round
to the tree house . . .

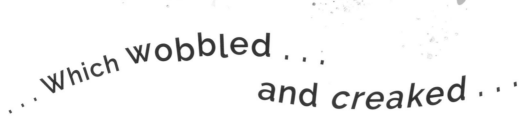

. . . Which wobbled . . .

and creaked . . .

and then someone said, "HI!"

A pink hairy face filled the tree house's window.
A big silver bottom poked out of the door.
A tail swished impatiently over the railing.
A clatter of hooves seemed to rattle the floor.

"At LAST!" cried a voice. "We've been waiting for AGES!"
"When do the crafts start? I've brought my 10p!"
"UNICORNS? Really?" gasped Amy, astounded.
"Of course," they all laughed. "Well, what else would we be?"

The smallest squeezed out and he slid down the ladder.
His glorious horn sparkled bright in the sun.
"I'm Legend," he whinnied and nuzzled her elbow.
"I reckon your Unicorn Club will be fun!"

So Amy thought fast: "You're too big for the tree house."
She ran to the garage and beckoned them in.

She got out the crayons and glitter and paint pots.
The unicorn crafts were about to begin!

They stomped and they sparkled on huge bits of paper.
They painted and pottered, and glittered and glued.

Then Legend got hungry: "What snacks are we having?"
And Amy rushed off to find unicorn food!

The unicorns crunched
and they snuffled and slobbered –
For magical beasts, they
weren't very polite –

Until they were done
and the food was demolished,
And then they licked Amy
with total delight.

"Okay," giggled Amy, "it's time for some dancing!
We've got some rosettes for the funkiest moves."
They wriggled and rocked and they rolled on the floorboards.
They discoed and cantered and kicked up their hooves.

"Fantastic!" said Amy. "I can't choose a winner.
Let's ALL have rosettes," and she handed them round.
The unicorns neighed and tossed their manes proudly.

But . . . "Oh!" – Amy saw something squashed on the ground.

"What's wrong?" Legend asked, trotting over to help her.
"My chalks!" Amy sniffed, staring into the tub.
"I wanted to brighten our den with a mural."
"Hang on . . ." Legend grinned, "this is UNICORN Club!"

He lowered his head and his horn started glowing. The air seemed to shimmer with colours and light.

Then WHOOSH!

they had brushes and jars full of rainbows!
They all got to work . . .

. . . and it soon looked **JUST RIGHT!**

So, Saturday morning was full of excitement!
Saturday morning turned out to be great.
The Unicorn Club is completely amazing.
They're meeting next weekend –
and Amy can't wait!

More **astounding** adventures from Little Tiger Press:

THE ONE-STOP STORY SHOP

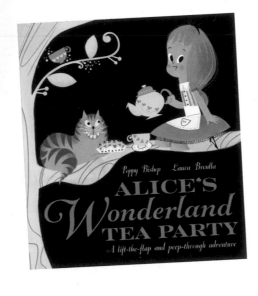

Peppy Bishop · Laura Brenlla

ALICE'S Wonderland TEA PARTY

A lift-the-flap and peep-through adventure

the SPACE TRAIN

Maudie Powell-Tuck · Karl James Mountford

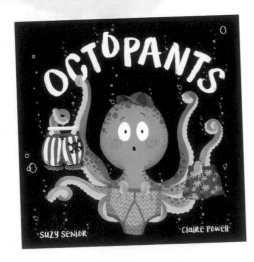

OCTOPANTS

SUZY SENIOR · CLAIRE POWELL

Linda Sunderland · Jessica Courtney-Tickle

SHHH! I'M READING!

JOHN KELLY · ELINA ELLIS

For information regarding any of the above titles
or for our catalogue, please contact us:
Little Tiger Press Ltd, 1 Coda Studios,
189 Munster Road, London SW6 6AW
Tel: 020 7385 6333 · E-mail: contact@littletiger.co.uk
www.littletiger.co.uk